LOVERS

LOVERS:

A Midrash

by
Edeet Ravel

NUAGE
EDITIONS

The author would like to express her gratitude to John Detre for his invaluable support and assistance.

Cover art by Gina Georgousis.
Cover design by Ramez Rabbat.
Photograph of Edeet Ravel by Uzi Witkowski.
Published with the assistance of The Canada Council.
Printed and bound in Canada by Imprimerie d'Edition Marquis Ltée.

Dépôt légal, Bibliothèque nationale du Québec and the
National Library of Canada.

Canadian Cataloguing in Publication Data

Ravel, Edeet, 1955–
    Lovers : a midrash

ISBN 0-921833-01-6

    I. Title.

PS8585.A8715L68 1994   C813' .54   C94-900792-7
PR9199.3.R38L68 1994

NuAge Editions, P.O. Box 8, Station E
Montréal, Québec, H2T 3A5

for Larissa

"Don't misunderstand me," said the priest. "I am only showing you the various opinions concerning that point. You must not pay too much attention to them. The scriptures are unalterable and the comments often enough merely express the commentator's bewilderment. In this case there even exists an interpretation which claims that the deluded person is really the doorkeeper."

"That's a far-fetched interpretation," said K. "On what is it based?"

Franz Kafka
The Trial

CONTENTS

The Sages

> Rav Huna
> ben Huna (Rav Huna's son)
> Zabdai
> Ephes ben Zabdai (Zabdai's son)
> Ukba from Babylon
> Resh Laqish

DEPARTURE

Rav Huna is annoyed with his son. His son has not answered the knock on his bedroom door three times this week, and once again Rav Huna must walk to the House of Study alone, leaning on his cane.

Rav Huna enters the House of Study, leans against the wall for support, and pulls off his boots. In the corner of the House of Study lies a newborn goat. No one is quite sure what it is doing there.

Resh Laqish is young and athletic. He swims in the river even in winter. Rav Huna's son sits on the bank of the river and watches Resh Laqish. Resh Laqish calls Rav Huna's son to join him, but Rav Huna's son refuses. He doesn't like dirt on his feet. And he doesn't like the cold. But he enjoys watching Resh Laqish, whose strong arms break the water with swift, determined strokes as he surges forward.

Zabdai arrives at the House of Study looking pale. He says, "I had a bad dream."

Resh Laqish says, "It may have been something you ate."

Ukba from Babylon says, "It may have been the Satan visiting you in your sleep."

Rav Huna says, "Perhaps it was the Satan, lodged in a piece of food."

Zabdai smiles. Nevertheless, his dream returns to him at intervals throughout the day.

Rav Huna says, "Jacob buried Rachel on the road to Ephrat because he knew that one day the exiles would walk down that road, their chains dragging upon the earth."

Rav Huna's son says, "And yet Rachel was deserving of eternal rest."

Rav Huna does not reply.

Zabdai stays up late in the House of Study. He likes the quiet and he likes the night. He can see the moon through the window and he can hear the sound of jackals howling in the forest. He is studying the verse in Ezekiel, "Son of man, shall these bones rise?"

He cannot decide which word to emphasize: *son* or *man.*

Zabdai says, "Man was created from clay."

Ukba from Babylon says, "The angels urged God to make man."

Rav Huna says, "Ukba is right. The angels were overwhelmed by Creation. They were hoping that with man it would come to an end."

Resh Laqish's wife steps down into the ritual bath. Under the water her hair sways like seaweed. She comes out of the bath, sits near the stove and lets the warm air dry her. She rubs her neck with oil and thinks of Resh Laqish. The voices of the other women remind her of small golden lizards sleeping in the sun.

Resh Laqish and Rav Huna's son stroll by the river at dusk. Resh Laqish says, "God has no power over the souls of men."

A friendly dog runs up to them. Rav Huna's son throws him a stick and says, "God has no power over the bodies of men."

Ukba from Babylon brings a large bowl of cheese to the House of Study. He says, "A wealthy man is a man who enjoys what he has."

Rav Huna's son says, "A wealthy man is a man who has seventeen vineyards, twenty-six servants and four wives."

Zabdai says, "Seventeen vineyards, twenty-six servants, four wives and a delicious bowl of cheese."

Zabdai's son has just turned nineteen. In the House of Study someone says, "Ephes ben Zabdai, when will the hand of a woman grasp the sturdy palm tree?"

Ephes ben Zabdai blushes. A stray cat jumps onto the window ledge of the House of Study and peers inside.

Ukba from Babylon, Zabdai and Rav Huna are dining together at Ukba's house. Ukba, a widower, has prepared an excellent meal: roasted chicken, almonds soaked in wine and two honey cakes. As they eat, Ukba from Babylon says, "Man consumes food and woman consumes man."

Rav Huna laughs. "Only if she deems him deserving, Ukba."

Zabdai smiles and helps himself to more cake. He has been married three times.

Zabdai says, "The first being was neither male nor female: the first being was a hermaphrodite. And when the Holy One revealed his plans for two separate beings, the hermaphrodite wept with the sorrow of a deserted lover."

Resh Laqish's wife sits at the table and kneads dough. The children chase one another through the house and under the table, shrieking with excitement. Every now and then a child's hand clutches fiercely at Resh Laqish's wife's skirt as though she were an oar in a shipwreck. But as the pursuer approaches, the child lets go of the skirt and flees.

Ukba from Babylon says, "A man without virtue is a pitiful thing."

But no one is listening. Zabdai and his son are discussing potential brides, Rav Huna is massaging his aching legs, Rav Huna's son is sitting in a corner reading, and Resh Laqish is wondering what his wife will prepare for dinner.

The days are growing colder. Resh Laqish climbs a ladder and spends the morning repairing the roof of his house. As he works, he imagines a lion creeping up on him from behind. He imagines a struggle from which he emerges victorious. The lion, tamed, sits at the front door and guards the house against evil.

The Sages enter the bath-house. Ukba from Babylon says, "Once a certain Sage was sitting in the bath-house. A Roman soldier came by and ordered him to move. The Roman soldier sat down in the place of the Sage and was immediately bitten by a snake. He died within minutes."

Rav Huna says, "Ukba will go straight to heaven, but he will never see the Holy One."

Ukba from Babylon says, "No one sees the Holy One, not even in heaven."

There is a story in which a man called Joseph finds a jewel inside a fish. Rav Huna thinks the story is childish but Ukba from Babylon likes it. He tells the story in the House of Study.

Rav Huna says, "You'll have the entire town looking for jewels in their fish. They will soon forget that the spirit of God is everywhere."

Rav Huna's son bursts out laughing.

Zabdai says, "The sun and the rain and the soul travel silently from one end of the earth to the other."

Rav Huna says, "You think the soul glides through heaven, but you're wrong. The soul breaks through heaven like a hammer shattering stone."

A storm erupts over the town and the rain comes pouring down.

Rav Huna enters the House of Study wet and shivering. He sits by the stove and a puddle of water forms at his feet. He says, "Of every hundred men who perish, ninety-nine perish of cold."

Zabdai brings two flasks of wine to the House of Study in celebration of the new month. Zabdai's son Ephes adds wood to the stove and pours the wine.

Resh Laqish says, "Time is the same for everyone but each man has his own chronology."

Zabdai says, "Death is the same for everyone, but each man has his own eternity."

Rav Huna says, "Inebriation is the same for everyone."

Ukba from Babylon says, "There was once a woman whose modesty was so great that her husband did not realize she had only one hand until she was dead."

Rav Huna's son feels that if he stays in the House of Study one minute longer he will be dead. He gets up, steps outside and looks out at the town. The idea of travel takes hold of him. He goes home, packs his belongings and returns to the House of Study to kiss his father and say good-bye.

Resh Laqish's wife digs in the garden and unearths two bones. It is a clear day: the sky is very blue. In the distance Resh Laqish's wife can see the House of Study. She imagines the House of Study soaring up to the sky and the men gliding down slowly, one by one, like large black birds.

Midrash on Song of Songs, 8:1-6

NEW YORK

O that it could be with you as with a brother

Shortly after my miscarriage, my husband had a party for the members of his orchestra.

"I can reschedule it," my husband said.

"No, I'd like to meet them," I said.

I was in the kitchen when the guests arrived. I was peering into the oven, my back facing the door. All at once I had an animal sense of danger. I turned and saw a very beautiful woman standing in the doorway, her dark coat dusted with a thin layer of snow.

I went into the bathroom and undressed. I lay in the bathtub, turned the hot water on with my toes, and thought, "That woman will want to use the bathroom. She'll be dressed and I'll be naked."

And sure enough, after about half an hour someone knocked on the door. It was the beautiful woman, wanting to come in, and I was naked and she was not.

who nursed at my mother's breasts

A week after my miscarriage I gave a lecture at the university. The lecture took place at the department of Islamic Studies. My husband sat in the back row.

After the lecture, Dr Anna Wing, the woman in charge of the lecture series, invited us for a drink.

An actor came by and sat at our table. In a show he'd seen the night before, he said, a woman had drawn a fish from under her skirt.

then if I met you in the streets

Before we became lovers, my husband told me about a beautiful woman who had spent the night with him. He said this was an unusual experience for him; he had never before slept with such a beautiful woman.

Two days after the party at our house I took a bath and thought about the beautiful woman in my husband's orchestra.

Then I remembered the beautiful woman who had spent the night with my husband before we were lovers. I thought, "It's probably not the same woman." Then I thought, "But why not? It could very well be her."

I would kiss you

My husband was reading in bed. I entered the bedroom and lay down beside him. I said, "Do you remember you once told me about a beautiful woman you slept with?"

But he said, "No."

So that was that.

and none would despise me

    I pulled all my diaries out of the closet and found the one I wrote the year I met my husband. I took the diary with me to work. All day, between classes and meetings, I searched through the diary for a reference to the conversation in which my husband told me about the beautiful woman who had spent the night with him.

    I hoped to find a clue that would reveal whether the beautiful woman in my husband's orchestra was the same woman with whom he'd spent the night. But though I read the diary twice, I found nothing about that particular conversation.

I would take you and lead you to my mother's house

Three weeks passed. I lay in my bed all day and listened to my husband moving in the next room.

I would quench your thirst

I went to a café with my girlfriend. At the other end of the room I saw Dancsak, my husband's agent. I went up to him and introduced myself.

"Ah," he said. He rose and shook my hand. "My pleasure," he said.

Of course the pleasure was mine. Now I would be able to tell my husband that I had met Dancsak.

with spiced wine

My husband and I drove to Boston to visit friends. On the way, my husband told me a story about a famous soprano. But I was mesmerized by the sight of his hands lying casually on the steering wheel, and as for his story, I heard only a series of sounds changing continuously in rhythm and pitch.

with the sweet juice of my pomegranates

I asked my husband about all the musicians in his orchestra. In this way I found out that the beautiful woman played the viola and that she had joined the orchestra only seven months ago. That explained why I had not seen her until now.

I said, "Did you know her before she joined the orchestra?"

My husband said, "I saw her around. She was a student at the school."

his left hand under my head

Before I met my husband he lived an isolated life. But at the music school everyone knew him and greeted him warmly when he walked down the halls.

My husband must have spoken to the viola player in the school lounge or at a reception or backstage after a student recital. Or he could have run into her at one of the many concerts and recitals he attended. They would have spotted each other during intermission and possibly made plans to meet after the show, go for a drink.

his right hand

    This is how it must have happened: they arranged to meet after the performance. Downstairs near the box office (now closed) they discussed where they could go for a drink. My husband had his car: they walked through the parking lot and by the time they were inside the car they already knew they would spend the night together.

caressing

At the beginning of April my husband's cousin from Louisiana phoned me. She was in town for Easter. In a few days her husband, a famous Louisiana lawyer, would be joining her. On the phone she told me she was pregnant.

I met her downtown. She said, "I have to find this man I once knew."

So we went to Spring Street, where he used to live, and we asked storekeepers in the area and waiters at a restaurant where he once worked and the roommate of a friend of his who lived nearby whether they knew where he'd gone. But no one could tell us.

My husband's cousin said, "I haven't seen him in six years."

"What does he look like?" I asked.

She said, "He looks like Apollo, he looks like Adonis."

O daughters of Jerusalem

I went to hear my husband's orchestra. I chose a seat with a good view of the strings, and I watched the beautiful woman as she looked up at my husband.

When the performance was over I went backstage and looked for the beautiful woman. But by the time I found the dressing room she'd already left.

I entreat you

On our way home from the concert hall I asked my husband, "Were you pleased with the players tonight?"

He said, "Some of the new ones were a bit off."

I said, "Can you really tell where each sound is coming from?"

My husband laughed. "Of course!" he said.

do not rouse or awaken love

One night my husband came home from an evening with some friends of his. He'd had a lot to drink. When he came to bed I began talking about the beautiful woman. I said, "I didn't like her performance dress. It made her look fat."

My husband said, "She has very large breasts. She wears loose clothes as a camouflage."

before my beloved is ready

The day after my husband told me about the beautiful woman's breasts I read an article in the newspaper about women with big breasts. The article listed the problems these women encountered because of the size of their breasts.

I clipped the column and read it a few times in the hope of finding a detail that would shed light on my husband's comment.

who is that coming up from the wilderness

My husband asked me whether I wanted to come to a poetry reading at the home of the beautiful woman. The beautiful woman's husband was going to read poetry from his latest book.

"I didn't know she was married," I said.

"But you met her husband. He was here at the party," my husband said.

"No, I missed him. Is he a good poet?"

"Well, he's published," my husband said.

"I'll come." I couldn't believe my luck.

leaning upon her beloved

When I had my miscarriage I stayed overnight at the hospital. In the next room a baby was crying, and as I slept, the cries entered my dreams, where they were transformed into a delicate piece of music played over and over solely for me.

under the apple tree

I tried to imagine the home of the beautiful woman. I imagined wooden floors and oak panelling and hand-woven rugs and small sophisticated sculptures on side-tables. I also imagined that I would see something startling and revealing that would settle all my questions at once. During the night, as I watched my husband sleep, I wondered what form this revelation could take.

I roused you

My husband spoke in his sleep. He said, "I love you."
I said, "You love me?"
"Yes," he answered, still asleep.

there your mother conceived you

It was late fall when my husband first fell in love with me. He led me to a secluded corner behind a church so he could kiss me. He said, "I don't know why I love you. You don't look anything like Isabelle Adjani." He was teasing me of course. I knew he was passionately in love with me.

there she who bore you conceived you

The apartment of the beautiful woman was in an old building. The elevator was out of order and there was an unpleasant smell in the stairwell. We walked up to the third storey and as we approached the beautiful woman's door, we could hear the voices of guests who had arrived before us. We knocked on the door and waited to be let in.

seal me in your heart

The beautiful woman took our coats and led us to the living room. The room was bare: there was nothing in it apart from seven folding chairs and a loveseat. Even the walls were bare; even the lightbulb was bare.

I sat on the loveseat and noticed a faded blood stain near my head. The beautiful woman was at the front door, welcoming other guests who had come to hear her husband's poetry. I looked again at the bare room. There was an overwhelming sense of sadness and violence in the air.

seal me upon your arm

The beautiful woman's husband came over and thanked us for coming. He was very tall and very thin and he had odd bird-like features. He looked a little mad.

Suddenly a blond child of six or seven with the same odd bird-like features appeared in the room. I did not think at first that he could possibly be the son of the beautiful woman. I assumed that he was her husband's son from a former marriage. Just then the boy spoke to the beautiful woman and addressed her as "mama." I asked my husband, "Is that her child?"

"Yes," he said.

The child brought a sleeping bag into the room and fell asleep in a corner by the loveseat. Had I reached over the arm of the loveseat I could have touched his hair, stroked his cheek. Now, looking at him as he slept, I saw the curves and outlines of the beautiful woman in his face. It was all I could do to keep myself from bending down and kissing him.

for love is as strong as death

Ten days before my miscarriage I dreamt the tiny queen of a tiny people had stolen my husband. When I came to rescue him, the tiny queen stabbed me with a knife. Of course the knife was so small I hardly noticed. I took the knife and stabbed the tiny queen back, killing her.

When I went to the hospital ten days later, they told me the embryo had been dead for ten days. I wasn't surprised; I had woken from the dream shivering with cold.

for love is as strong as death

Towards the end of April my husband and I drove up to the mountains.

We stopped near a lake and walked along the shore.

There were thin sheets of ice on the lake, but along the edges the water was a deep blue. Everything was still and quiet.

"I could lie down here and sleep for days," I said. I felt happy and at peace.

ABSENCE

Rav Huna is sick. His vision is blurred, his joints are swollen, his bowels are not functioning properly. Zabdai comes to visit Rav Huna and brings him a bowl of stew. It is early spring and the smell of fig trees in bloom drifts in through the window.

Zabdai says, "Today in the House of Study Resh Laqish was speaking of justice."

Rav Huna says, "What a coincidence. All day today my body was speaking to me of injustice."

Zabdai changes the subject.

Zabdai's son Ephes has chosen a bride. The wedding is large and festive. When it is over, Zabdai and his wife go home. Ephes has built an addition to his father's house, with a separate entrance. As he is about to go in, Resh Laqish draws him aside and says, "Remember, ben Zabdai, a wild horse runs for pleasure, even if it has never seen a man or felt a saddle on its back."

Resh Laqish and his wife put the children to sleep and eat a late meal. Resh Laqish's wife asks Resh Laqish to pick her a few apricots for dessert. He steps outside into the dark warm night. His wife stands in the doorway, watching him. The cold, wet grass tickles his ankles. A soft breeze blows his wife's nightgown against her legs.

Ukba from Babylon says, "In Eden there were hairy beasts shaped like humans. When Adam and Eve sinned, the Holy One gave them the skins of the beasts."

Resh Laqish says, "Maybe it was the other way around. Maybe he gave the beasts the skins of Adam and Eve."

Rav Huna says, "You would like to think so, Resh Laqish."

Rav Huna says, "Three in a room may discuss Creation."
Zabdai says, "Two before nightfall may discuss Creation."
A gentle snore is heard in the House of Study. Ephes ben Zabdai, newly married, has fallen asleep.

Ukba from Babylon says, "The Satan lives in Gehenna."

Resh Laqish says, "The Satan has no form."

Rav Huna says, "The Satan has come up for a visit. He's clutching at my leg."

Zabdai says, "The moon was created for women."

Later that day he says, "The moon was not created for women. The moon was created for thieves."

A desert wind blows through the town. In the House of Study, Zabdai's son Ephes sweeps the sand from the table.

Resh Laqish says, "Moses should not have hidden his face when he heard God's voice. God would have shown him everything, but he hid his face."

Resh Laqish comes home from the House of Study and finds that his wife has lit all the lamps. It is still light out: the days are growing longer.

Resh Laqish wonders what demons his wife has had to chase away. He turns and sees her through the window, scattering grain for the chicken.

Ukba from Babylon says, "Job lived in the days of Jacob."
Zabdai says, "Job lived in the days of the judges."
Rav Huna says, "Job lived in the days of the judged."

Ukba from Babylon dreams about an enormous frog. On the following day he says, "The plague of frogs came about in this way: one enormous frog gave birth to thousands of little frogs."

Zabdai laughs. "Or perhaps one enormous frog whistled and thousands of little frogs came running."

Resh Laqish says, "Or perhaps one enormous frog sent out invitations and thousands of little frogs replied."

Rav Huna smiles. It is a beautiful day and everyone is in high spirits.

Rav Huna leaves his house and takes a path that leads to the forest. The sound of children reaches him through the trees. He follows the sound until he reaches a small clearing. Resh Laqish's wife, surrounded by her children, stirs fresh mushrooms in a pan set over a small fire. Rav Huna leans on his cane and waits for her to notice him, for quite suddenly a ravenous desire for the smooth and slippery taste of cooked mushrooms has seized him.

The Sages are discussing the verse *By the waters of Babylon we sat and wept.*

Zabdai says, "They wept because they were naked."

Rav Huna says, "They wept because even though they were naked, they were forced by their captors to play their harps."

Resh Laqish brings his little daughter to the House of Study.

Rav Huna says, "Five in a room may discuss Creation."

Zabdai says, "Life is a shadow cast by a wall."

Resh Laqish says, "Life is a shadow cast by a bird."

Rav Huna says, "Life is a shadow cast by a bird upon the shadow cast by a wall."

The question arises in the House of Study: How many plagues did God inflict on the Pharaoh? Zabdai says twenty. Ukba from Babylon says thirty. Rav Huna looks out the window and says six hundred and thirty. The Sages turn to look out the window as well. There is the usual view: the dirt road that leads to the House of Study.

Midrash on Song of Songs, 8:1-6

LONDON

O that it could be with you as with a brother

Two impecunious ugly sisters looking for beaux who will wine
and dine us. Our gratitude shall know no bounds.

Box 6023

who nursed at my mother's breasts

To Box 6023:
We are two chaps, 14 and 15, who would be honoured to wine
and dine you in return for bennefitting from your vast
experience, particularly in the field of sexual intercoarse. We
look forward to hearing from you fairly soon.

then if I met you in the streets

O! Blessed Sisters:
Ho, every one who thirsts, come to the waters;
and he who has no money,
come, buy and eat!
Come, buy wine and milk without money and without price.
Eat what is good, and delight yourself in fatness.
Come to me;
hear, that your soul may live!

I would kiss you

Dear Advertisers:

and none would despise me

Boris. 555-1265

I would take you and lead you to my mother's house

To The Hungry And Thirsty Women
Consider this:
Once there was an old man who asked a Buddhist scholar:
"Which has a broader meaning: the *so* commentaries, or the *sho* commentaries that explain the *so?*"
The scholar said, "*Sho* explains the *so* and *so* explains the text."
The old man said, "What does the text explain?"
The scholar was speechless!

I would quench your thirst

If thou beest born to strange sights,
Things invisible to see,
Ride ten thousand days and nights,
Till age snow white hairs on thee.
Thou, when thou return'st, wilt tell me
All strange wonders that befell thee
And swear
Nowhere
Lives **a woman true**, and fair.
If thou find'st one, **let me know**,
Such a pilgrimage were sweet;
Yet do not, I would not go,
Though at **next** door **we might meet**;
Though she were true when you met her,
And last till you **write your letter,**
Yet she
Will be
False, **ere I come**, to two, or three.

with spiced wine

My Good Mesdames,

I am pleased to make your acquaintance. Myself and my friend are in great need of English and correct correspondence. If you wish to wine and dine, the pleasure is ours. We look forward to your hasty reply and thank you for your kind attention.

with the sweet juice of my pomegranates

To Box 6023:

In our last correspondance, we expressed hopes of bennefitting from your vast experience. We apologize most sinceerly if we offended you. Of course, we are aware that you have much to offer quite apart from sexual intercoarse and we anxiously await your generous reply.

his left hand under my head

O! Blessed Sisters:
Whereas you have been forsaken and hated,
with no one passing through,
I will make you majestic forever,
a joy from age to age.
You shall suck the milk of nations,
You shall suck the breasts of kings!

his right hand

Boris. (07) 555-1265

caressing

To The Hungry And Thirsty Women
Consider this:
Kanzan the poet asked Master Bukan, "If an ancient mirror is not polished, how can it reflect the light of a candle?"
Bukan said, "A crystal vessel filled with ice has no shadow. A monkey will reach out to touch the moon when it appears in a pond."
Kanzan said, "These things do not reflect light. Will you persist with your talk?"
Bukan said, "If these are of no help, what do you want me to say?"
Kanzan bowed and withdrew.

O daughters of Jerusalem

Call us what you will, we're made such by **love**;
Call her one, **me** another fly,
We're tapers too, and at our own cost die,
And we in us find th' eagle and the dove.
The phoenix riddle hath more wit
By us: we two being one, are it.
So, to one neutral thing both **sexes** fit.
We die and rise the same, and **prove**
Mysterious by this love.

I entreat you

Dear Distinguished Mesdames,

We refer to our letter formerly, which has perhaps not found a correct address. We are two gentlemen in great need of English. If you would care to meet, we wish only to have exquisite conversation. A restaurant of your choosing will be our pleasure. We thank you for your kind attention and we look forward to your reply.

do not rouse or awaken love

We are the two chaps who have written previously. We forgot to mention that I will be 16 next week while my friend, Goodwin, will be happy to act as shaperone for the time being.

p.s. We are both in public school.

before my beloved is ready

O! Unrepentent Sisters:
I have trodden the wine press alone,
and from the peoples no one was with me;
I trod them in my anger
and trampled them in my wrath;
their lifeblood is sprinkled upon my garments,
and I have stained all my rainment.
For the day of vengeance was in my heart.
I trod down the peoples in my anger
and I poured out their lifeblood on the earth!

who is that coming up from the wilderness

To The Hungry And Thirsty Women
Consider this:
Master Unmon had once quoted Master Baso as saying, "Daiba treated all words with respect; this is an important thing."
Then Unmon said, "This is a fine saying, but nobody has asked me anything about it."
At that, a monk asked, "What is the Daiba sect?"
Unmon said, "There are 96 heretical schools in India, and you belong to the lowest one."

leaning upon her beloved

Like pictures, or like books' gay coverings made
For lay-men, are all **women** thus arrayed;
Themselves are mystic books, which only we
(Whom their imputed grace will dignify)
Must see revealed. Then, since that I may know,
As liberally as to a midwife, **show**
Thyself: cast all, yea, this white linen hence,
There is no penance due to innocence.

under the apple tree

Our Dearest Mesdames,
We have found no reply as of today to our letters of a bygone time. We are gentleman of repute and distinction in great need of English. We yearn with hope to make your acquaintance and our wish is only to be for your disposal. Words cannot say how deeply we await your most kind reply.

I roused you

My God, my God
Why hast thou forsaken me?
Why?

there your mother conceived you

To The Hungry And Thirsty Women
Since you will not reply, consider this:
Master Isan saw the nun Ryutetsuma coming. He greeted her,
saying, "Here you are, old cow!"
Ryutetsuma said, "Tomorrow there is going to be a dinner
meeting at Mount Tai. Is Your Reverend going?"
Isan lay down in a sleeping posture.
Ryutetsuma departed.

there she who bore you conceived you

To our bodies turn we then, that so
Weak men on love revealed **may** look;
Love's mysteries in souls do grow,
But yet the body is his book.
And if some lover, such as we,
Have heard **this dialogue of one,**
Let him **still** mark us; he shall see
Small **change** when we're to bodies gone.

seal me in your heart

Gentle Mesdames,
We are the gentlemen who have written to you beforetimes of our great need of English. Please find enclosed a photograph for your perusal. We hope greatly to find you amenable. Eagerly we thank you for your kindest and humble attention.

seal me upon your arm

Here, take my picture; though I bid **farewell**,
Thine, in my heart, where my soul dwells, shall dwell.
'Tis like me now, but I dead, 'twill be more
When we are shadows both, than 'twas before.
When weather-beaten I com back, my hand,
Perhaps with **rude** oars torn, or sunbeams tanned,
My face and breast of haircloth, and my head
With care's rash sudden storms being o'erspread,
My body'a **sack of bones**, broken within,
And powder's blue stains scattered on my skin;
If rival fools tax thee to have loved a man
So foul and coarse as, Oh, I may seem then,
This shall say what I was.

for love is as strong as death

Dearest Mesdames,
Please find enclosed a cheque for your transportation to our hotel. We are in great need of English and do not wish you to have superfluous expense. We wish you happiness and await your reply.

for love is as strong as death

Dear Kindest Mesdames,
We thank you greatly for your kind reply. We look forward to making your acquaintance at 7 o'clock at the Savoy Hotel, as you have expressed so well.

RETURN

Rav Huna's son returns from his journey with a manual of astrology, five birds, and many gifts. He enters the House of Study and embraces his father.

Rav Huna says, "The explorer has returned."

Ukba from Babylon says, "We were speaking of the parting of the Red Sea."

Rav Huna's son says, "Please come to my house this evening. I have presents for everyone." Then he leaves.

The discussion of the parting of the Red Sea is not resumed.

Rav Huna's son has built a small aviary for his birds. At night he studies his manuals of astrology and in the early morning he lies in bed and tries to distinguish the birdcalls within and around his house. He has been to the House of Study only twice since his return.

Rav Huna's son, Resh Laqish and Ephes ben Zabdai climb the mountain to the east of the town. When they reach the top they sit on the rocks and eat bread, oranges and black grapes. Rav Huna's son looks out at the clear blue sky and says, "What if God sees the House of Study only through us?"

Resh Laqish says, "The Queen of Sheba asked Solomon to interpret the words *day* and *night* by means of numerology."

Rav Huna says, "The Queen of Sheba asked Solomon to interpret the words *darkness* and *silence* by means of numerology."

Zabdai says, "The Queen of Sheba asked Solomon to lift the hem of her skirt as she crossed the floor of his palace. The crystal floor was so clear and luminous that the Queen of Sheba mistook it for a pool of clear water."

Resh Laqish stays up late with Zabdai in the House of Study. The room is lit by a single lamp and the men cannot see each other clearly.

Resh Laqish says, "In the beginning death is a cobweb. In the end death is the rope one ties to a ship."

Zabdai says, "In the beginning death is a guest. In the end death is the host."

Ukba from Babylon says, "Joseph had arranged a romantic tryst with Potiphar's wife. It was only at the very last minute that he changed his mind."

Zabdai says, "Joseph was seduced by his own beauty. One's own beauty is even more tempting than that of another."

Resh Laqish looks up at Zabdai with astonishment. For the rest of the day he is silent.

Zabdai says, "The mountains were created for the wild goats."

Rav Huna says, "And the stars, apparently, were created for my son."

Resh Laqish says, "Perhaps the stars really were created for the astrologers."

Rav Huna looks at Resh Laqish sharply and says, "Men are not goats."

Resh Laqish and his wife lie in bed at night. The room is filled with the sounds of crickets and jackals. One of Rav Huna's son's owls hoots in the darkness.

Rav Huna's joints are getting worse. He sits with his legs resting on an empty chair. He says, "When a man dies, his soul mourns for him."

Ukba from Babylon says, "His soul mourns for seven days."

Zabdai says, "A soul has no sense of time."

Resh Laqish says, "A soul has no sense of sorrow."

Rav Huna's son sets out to visit Resh Laqish. As he passes the bathhouse, he hears the voice of a man singing. He peeps through a crack in the door and sees Ukba from Babylon sitting regally in the bathhouse by himself, singing a love song. His voice is rich and melodious and full of emotion. Rav Huna's son stands quietly by the door until the song is finished.

Resh Laqish visits Rav Huna's son at dusk and sees an astrology book open on the table. He sits down at the table and says, "Ben Huna, do your charts really reveal the future?"

Rav Huna's son says, "They reveal the past, and the past reveals the future."

Resh Laqish leans back in the chair and looks at Rav Huna's son. A euphoric sense of intimacy settles quietly over them in the darkening room. If he could, Rav Huna's son would take Resh Laqish in his arms.

Rav Huna says, "When the time comes, the Holy One will unleash the sun and it will burn the earth."

Ukba from Babylon says, "Gehenna will rise up and burn the earth."

Zabdai says, "Neither the sun nor Gehenna will burn the earth. Man himself will turn into fire and burn the earth."

Zabdai says, "The light of the Messiah was created from dew."

Zabdai's son stands up and says, "That reminds me. I promised my wife I'd be home early."

Ukba from Babylon says, "Vanity of vanities: a man plants a tree and another man eats its fruit."

Rav Huna says, "Vanity of vanities: a man reads a verse and understands neither the first word nor the last."

Zabdai goes down to the river and sees Resh Laqish's youngest daughter lose her balance and fall into the water. She sinks instantly. Zabdai runs along the bank, jumps in, and pulls her out. The little girl coughs, rubs her eyes, and runs away before Zabdai can rebuke her.

Zabdai does not tell Resh Laqish about the incident.

Rav Huna says, "Abraham knew he had reached the place where Isaac was to be sacrificed when on the third evening, just before sunset, a great cloud swept down upon the mountain and lay before him, as still and immovable as a shroud."

Rav Huna's son sits under a tree and eats bread and cheese and olives and dates. It is a hot day and all around him the crickets are buzzing. There is no question about it: the sound of the crickets comes from below, not from above.

Midrash on Song of Songs, 8:1-6

JERUSALEM

O that it could be with you as with a brother

To reach my house you must first enter a small courtyard enclosed by four walls. To enter the courtyard, you must open a heavy iron gate; the gate divides the wall that separates the courtyard from the street. The landlady's house is on the north side of the courtyard, immediately on your right as you enter through the gate. I live in the house adjacent to hers. Across the courtyard, facing the landlady's house, live an elderly couple who are relatives of the landlady, and in the house next to them, a student. But whereas my house is adjacent to the landlady's house, the two houses on the south side of the courtyard are separate structures. They are not entirely independent, however, for the relatives' house is attached to the east wall of the courtyard, and the student's house is attached to the west wall.

I am in love with the student.

who nursed at my mother's breasts

I say houses, but they are really simple stone structures, each with a window on one side and a door in front. In my house I have a bed, a table, two chairs, a dresser, a refrigerator, a sink, and a Primus stove. The landlady washes the floors of all four houses every day. This is not part of an agreement reached between her and the tenants. She washes the floors because they are hers.

then if I met you in the streets

The houses are old. The landlady was born in hers. I asked her, didn't you ever want to travel, change your surroundings, see new sights? She said that there have been many dramatic changes right there in the courtyard: plumbing, electricity, the new outhouse. And then the long procession of tenants who have lived in these houses over the years. Not to mention all that she herself has been through during her life. Then she smiled and told me to wait a moment. She entered her house and emerged with a bowl of vine leaves stuffed with rice. "You're too thin," she said as she handed me the bowl. Then she threw her head back and laughed.

I would kiss you

    Between the student's house and the relatives' house there is a combination outhouse and shower. In the winter we didn't use the shower; we heated water on our stoves and washed near the kerosene heaters. But two weeks ago the last rain fell and all at once the weather has changed. Even the nights are already warm. Now each morning I see the student walk to the shower, a towel around his waist. The towel serves only to cover him, for he comes out of the shower wet, hair and beard dripping, eyes half-shut, the towel back in place. He leaves his door open, but because his house is nearer to the west wall than mine, I can't see into his room. So I don't know whether he dries himself indoors, or whether he waits until the water that remains on his body evaporates into the air.

and none would despise me

To enter the courtyard you must first unlock the heavy iron gate in the centre of the east wall. The wall is high, and crowned with shards of broken bottles to discourage intruders. The shards are decorative too, especially when they glitter in the sun and the different colours and shapes resemble the patterns seen through a kaleidoscope. I often wonder whether this beauty is arranged or accidental. The landlady sees me looking at the glass shards and assures me that the lock on the gate is sturdy and that, in any case, she is a light sleeper, and would be sure to hear if anyone tried to break in.

I would take you and lead you to my mother's house

After the student has his shower I unlock the iron gate and leave for work. I am away for six hours. When I return in the afternoon, the student is gone. I find the landlady sweeping the courtyard, hanging laundry, watering the plants. Her relatives sit at a small table by their door and play backgammon. I close my shutters and fall into a deep sleep. At four I have tea and biscuits, and then I leave again to do errands. I try to be back for seven, because that is when the student usually comes home. We exchange a polite greeting and he disappears into his house. I can hear him rustling papers and a little later the sweet smell of hashish fills the courtyard. At times he goes out late in the evening and when he returns I am already asleep.

I would quench your thirst

The landlady offered to henna my hair. I sat on a chair outside my house and the landlady pounded the henna and massaged it into my hair. The henna made my hair sticky and lumpy: I felt like Medusa as I sat in the sun and waited for the colour to take effect. The landlady sat on a chair facing me and asked about my work. She told me the student is engaged to a woman in his village; apparently they have been engaged since his birth, or possibly hers, the landlady was not sure which. But she doubts that he will ever marry the woman. "He's left that life behind," she said. She dipped a tin cup into a pail of warm water and began rinsing my hair. The courtyard tiles turned a rusty red as the water poured down over them. "I like having young tenants," the landlady said, running her fingers through my hair. "I hope you'll stay."

with spiced wine

The nights are hot now, and we both sleep with our doors open. Early this morning the wails of the women praying in the distance woke me up and I couldn't get back to sleep. It was still dark out. I entered the courtyard and slowly walked to his doorway. I peered inside. When my eyes became accustomed to the dark I saw that he was lying naked on his back. I watched him until the outlines of objects began to emerge under an inky blue light and then I returned quickly to my room.

with the sweet juice of my pomegranates

On very hot days I shower twice: in the afternoon before my nap and in the evening before bed. I always undress in the showerhouse. My showers are long and expensive: I watch the meter ticking away. The landlady keeps track of the meter and tells us what we owe her when she collects the rent. When I'm through I wrap myself in a long robe and I carry my clothes back to my house. Sometimes when I come out of the shower I see him leaning in his doorway, taking a breath of air.

his left hand under my head

He has come to my house. At eight he appeared at my door just as I was about to sit down to eat, and asked whether he could boil water on my stove: his is broken. He boiled water, made strong coffee, and we drank together at the table. We said very little. I offered him a sandwich, he refused, smiled, finished his coffee and left.

his right hand

    To reach my house you must first enter a small courtyard. The floor of the courtyard is made of white tiles, but grass and weeds have pushed their way up between the tiles. Along the west wall there is a long narrow bench lined with potted plants and in the corner of the courtyard between my house and the bench a series of cords form the clotheslines. If I look out my window I can see his white shirts swaying in the breeze.

caressing

He now comes to my room every evening for coffee, even though his stove has been repaired. I tell him about my work in agricultural research and the science of seeds, and he tells me about his dissertation on states of emergency and the laws governing them. He has lent me a book of poetry. When he has time, he says, we will go see a movie together.

O daughters of Jerusalem

This morning he came out of his house with a small knapsack and said he was going away for a few days. I don't know where he has gone. I don't know how long he will be away.

I entreat you

    The days are long. I had three days off. On the first day I went to the sea and sat in the sun on a rented chair, watching the swimmers. It was noisy and crowded. I drank bottled water and sucked on lemon icicles I bought from a vendor who passed regularly between the chairs. I slept at a hotel on the beach: I did not want to go home. On the second day I went south to visit friends and stayed with them overnight. On the third day I came home and did not go out.

do not rouse or awaken love

I am trying to capture in my mind his expression when we say good night: it is as though he feels decisive about some indecision, and is amused at the contradiction.

before my beloved is ready

In the afternoon, when the landlady and her relatives were asleep, I entered his room. Books, papers, notebooks, heaps of clothes, empty bottles on the floor. On the wall various posters and a large map of the region. I opened the desk drawers. Pencils, pens, bills, receipts, hashish, stamps, a knife, a bottle opener, loose change, a magnifying glass, matches and a piece of paper with a few words scrawled on it in Arabic. I held the note in my hand and stared at it. The unlikely, decorative script filled me with unbearable desire. It seemed to me that if I could only decipher the sinuous markings on the page, I would be able to unlock the secret of my longing. I sat on the unmade bed, and held the bedclothes to my face. After a while I lay down and fell asleep. No one saw me when I left the room later.

who is that coming up from the wilderness

I returned to his room before I went to work. In a bottom drawer I found two more interesting items: a letter from a woman, and a gun. The letter is not dated and there is no return address, only her signature, Maria. But in her letter she writes about mountains, waterfalls and a damp cabin: images of a remote landscape.

leaning upon her beloved

The waiting is almost unbearable. I went out walking late at night, but the patrol picked me up, lectured me, and took me home.

under the apple tree

He came back yesterday just before midnight. I was already in bed but I was not asleep. He came into my room and when he saw that I was awake he said someone had been through his things.

I looked up at him in the dark and said, "How was I to know you would be coming back?" Then I moved over to make room for him in my bed.

I roused you

    To reach my house you must first enter a small courtyard. The landlady's relatives sit in the courtyard all day. The woman wears thick glasses and a kerchief on her head. The man's hands tremble slightly, but he is quite sharp when it comes to backgammon. I played with him a few times and he won consistently, though apologetically. In the afternoon I am surrounded by the aged. I sit in the courtyard and wait for night.

there your mother conceived you

At dusk everything changes. The landlady and her relatives retreat into their homes and the voices of television news broadcasters, low and urgent, begin to drift into the courtyard. The street noises are different too: the blare of traffic is replaced by loud conversations, shouts, and an occasional laugh, and the sound of military planes circling overhead becomes more distinct. When it is very hot at night, time loses all meaning.

there she who bore you conceived you

He tells me about his life. We lie in bed, in the heat, late into the night. In the afternoon I sometimes meet him at the university. He has many friends, and every now and then we join small gatherings in someone's house. At these gatherings we eat, listen to music and talk: the conversation strays from subject to subject, but can never escape the relentless shadow of politics. Everyone reclines on pillows and I rest my head on his legs.

seal me in your heart

I went to town in the morning and bought a skirt, new sandals, five new books, a silk bedspread and, for the landlady, a tablecloth. When I came home the landlady told me that the student had been arrested. At first she said soldiers had come to arrest him, but she was confused, and later she said the police had come. I turned to look at his door. The landlady said that they'd been in his room but she'd tidied up afterwards. I opened the door to his room and looked inside. The room was almost empty. His books and papers were gone. What was left behind had been passionately and meticulously arranged by the landlady: can opener, toothbrush, hairbrush, a bar of soap, a pair of sneakers, small change, cutlery, plates, glasses, pots and pans. It was a ghostly order, the sort that follows utter chaos. I could not tell whether the landlady had set the room in order out of defiance or compassion.

seal me upon your arm

I set out for the police station early in the morning, but while I was waiting for the bus a man who looked vaguely familiar came up to me, handed me a folded sheet of paper and disappeared into the crowd. I found a bench and sat down to look at the message. An address in Athens and a date, ten days from today. Nothing else. So instead of spending the morning at the police station, I arranged for a flight. I leave in four days.

for love is as strong as death

    I told the landlady I was leaving and paid our rent for the month. I also tried to give notice at work: I said I didn't know when I'd be back. But my employer insisted on saving the position for me, and said he would consider my absence a holiday leave.

for love is as strong as death

The landlady watched me as I packed my valise. I thought of her watching all the tenants who have passed through her courtyard as they unpacked, set up housekeeping, and then eventually packed up again to leave. When I was finished she invited me into her house for a parting tea. She had put on the tablecloth I bought for her and she thanked me again. She served cake and cookies and mint tea made with fresh leaves. The green stems filled the glass cup; the tea was sweet and delicious. We sat and drank, then I stood up to go. The landlady crossed her arms and looked at me. I could see that she wanted to tell me something, but had decided against it.

Song of Songs 8: 1-6

O that it could be with you as with a brother
    who nursed at my mother's breast!
Then if I met you in the streets, I would kiss you,
    and none would despise me.

I would take you
    and lead you to my mother's house
I would quench your thirst with spiced wine
    with the sweet juice of my pomegranates.

His left hand under my head,
    his right hand caressing.

O daughters of Jerusalem,
    I entreat you
Do not rouse or awaken love
    before my beloved is ready.

Who is that coming from the wilderness
    leaning upon her beloved?
Under the apple tree
    I roused you
There your mother conceived you
    there she who bore you conceived you.

Seal me in your heart
    seal me upon your arm
For love is as strong as death
    as cruel as the grave.

Afterword

The background text of Edeet Ravel's *Lovers: A Midrash* comes from the Song of Songs. The Song of Songs is unique among the books of the Bible in containing neither laws nor narrative history nor prophetic admonition. Rather, it appears to be a highly erotic love poem, so that one may well question how it entered the biblical canon. Though theories abound about the purpose, origin and conception of the Song of Songs, it has been suggested that the work belongs to a genre of ancient Near Eastern poetry written for recital during the sexual act—intended both to enhance physical pleasure and to raise the experience to a spiritual level. The lover's voice alternates between the male and female participant; the woman tells the man of his beauty and desirability, and he responds. Both use images of egress and regress, of closure and entrance, of withdrawal and loss followed by reunion—all suggesting intensely erotic content.

Even though both the language and the imagery of the Song of Songs are highly erotic, this erotic content has often been explained away. The text has been read by Christian interpreters, for example, as an allegory of God's relationship with the Church or the human soul. Their attempts to spiritualize the text—and to desexualize it—can be seen as one of the ways in which a patriarchal tradition has deprived women of the tenderly sensual aspects of their sexuality. Ironically, this also cuts off male sexuality as a physical entity at its source and thus emasculates even the spiritual and intellectual channels through which the senses can blossom.

There is another way, however, of reading the biblical text—the way of midrash. When you tell a story to explain another story, and in doing so suggest that your story must be explained by yet another story, you are using a kind of interpretative strategy that was commonly practised by the ancient rabbis. These rabbinic interpretations, which thrived in the first centuries of the first millennium of the Common Era, are known as midrash. *Midrash* is simply the Hebrew word for interpretation or explanation.

In theory, any passage from the Bible, whether from the books of the Laws or from the narrative or poetic parts, could be subjected to the midrashic process. For the midrashic scholars, gaps and ambiguity in the biblical text are there in order to beckon the readers and stir them to participation in the search for meaning. Thus, the practice of explaining a story by means of midrash brings out aspects of the primary story that might otherwise have remained hidden.

But midrash is far more than mere story; it is a way of reading that stands in radical opposition to any concept of knowledge as finite, closed, unambiguous or bound by syllogistic logic. Midrash is timeless. In midrash, past, present and future are one. The word is not separate from the divine world; the biblical text represents the whole of human experience. Every part of the biblical text, and hence, the world, is connected to every other part. To be understood, the words on a page must be expanded, played with and interpreted again and again, for truth is a process of endlessly deciphering meaning.

Lovers: A Midrash presents the reader with a verbal vision— or sequence of visions—and a puzzle, calling upon the reader to sense and think simultaneously. The text is divided into six parts, three of which (Departure, Absence, and Return) are written in the third person and focus on three Sages and their respective sons. Each of these three parts is followed by a

154

midrash on Song of Songs 8: 1-6 related in the first person by a contemporary female narrator. The third midrash (Jerusalem)—the final part of the book—is the culmination of the narrative as commentary. It is in this section that one realizes fully that this is a set of love stories.

The three traditional sections are concerned with the timeless world of the three Sages and their sons. The exegetes who engaged in midrash were, as far as we know, universally male. While maintaining this tradition, Ravel also plays with it, assigning names to her Sages which are drawn from different generations. Although these sections belong to the third-person masculine patriarchal order, even here the feminine pervades, first in the strong presence of Resh Laqish's wife, and then through the suggestion of a relationship of desire between Resh Laqish and the adventurous, scholarly and far-travelling son of Rav Huna. These traditional parts are about love, since they are about the love of study and intricate and teasing debate, about love for a circumscribed world and way of life. But even here one finds the physicality of the senses and the concreteness of imagination. This is a world of looking, seeing, and touching secretly. It is a world of vision that is also mediated through and through by language, the articulation that connects one area of the surface—of world, of time, of the page—with another.

The contemporary sections are reminiscent of Kundera in *The Unbearable Lightness of Being,* though on a much smaller scale. And just as Kundera's novel retells and modifies Tolstoi's *Anna Karenina,* so this part of Ravel's work gives a new meaning to the continuity and relevance of midrash. It helps us to reread the Songs of Songs in all its fresh, sensual immediacy and, in spite of the long tradition of rabbinic and Christian allegorizing, to realize that love belongs to sex and spirit together. By telling a set of contemporary stories that are sustained by the ancient biblical love song, Ravel breaks through centuries-old patriarchal defences and allows the voice of woman's tenderness and passion to be heard.

Much of postmodern writing breaks down the divisions among literary genres and features three particular traits: a strong sense of the tangible, indeed sensual, images of the world as verbal and textual phenomenon, a stress on the immediacy of language as writing and, in certain local literatures, the emergence of a tangential and indirect kind of allegory. The first of these traits is clearly present in Latin American writing, while the last is evident in a good deal of the literature coming from the recent past of eastern Europe. The middle trait—the consciousness of *écriture*—is generally pervasive. All of these characteristics are embodied in Ravel's work, in which she plays freely with the reader's expectations about time sequence, plot, and narrative structure.

In recent literary theories of allegory, the older model of secret meanings and depth analysis has been replaced by an understanding of the ingenious relationships that can be forged among very disparate sites, as well as the lacunae that these relations cast into relief. In many ways this is a return to something like the ancient tradition of midrash. It is the significant achievement of Ravel's work that she has enacted this recuperation in a fascinating, vibrant and accessible form.

Richard Cooper
Montreal, 1994

About the Author

Edeet Ravel was born on a kibbutz in Israel and moved to Montreal with her parents when she was seven years old. While studying in Jerusalem many years later, Ravel met the Israeli concert pianist Yaron Ross. They married and made London their base as they travelled Europe and the United States. In 1978 Ravel returned to Montreal, and presently lives in Deux Montagnes with her daughter Larissa.

Ravel won her first writing prize at the age of sixteen for a story which was published in the textbook *Telling Tales*. Later stories were included in the anthologies *Saturday Night at the Forum* and *Matinées Daily*. Parts of Ravel's *Lovers: A Midrash* have appeared in various literary journals, both in English and in Hebrew, and a collection of her children's stories about divorce is currently being made into a film. Ravel teaches Hebrew literature at McGill University.